THE LOOK-ALIKE GROOM

MAIL ORDER BRIDES OF CULVER'S CREEK

SUSANNAH CALLOWAY

Tica House
Publishing

Sweet Romance that Delights and Enchants!

PERSONAL WORD FROM THE AUTHOR

Dearest Readers,

Thank you so much for choosing one of my books. I am proud to be a part of the team of writers at Tica House Publishing who work joyfully to bring you stories of hope, faith, courage, and love. Your kind words and loving readership are deeply appreciated.

I would like to personally invite you to sign up for updates and to become part of our **Exclusive Reader Club**—it's completely Free to join! We'd love to welcome you!

Much love,

Susannah Calloway

VISIT HERE to Join our Reader's Club and to Receive Tica House Updates!

https://wesrom.subscribemenow.com/

CONTENTS

CHAPTER 1

The wedding was beautiful, but it cost Liliana Elison her last bit of strength to keep a smile on her face until it was over.

It wasn't that she was unhappy that her childhood friend had finally married the man she'd been engaged to for well over two years. Such a long engagement of twenty-six months — why, it seemed a lifetime – was the cause of speculation. Lili was so perfectly placed between the two parties as to know well what the cause of the delay was. Though everyone blamed it upon Gerald Hapstay, as he was an enlisted man and dependent upon the army's willingness to grant him leave, the fault really belonged at the doorstep of the Brown household. Most specifically, Mrs. Brontelle Brown, Anne's mother. Anne Brown was an only child, and her mother found it difficult to allow her to untie the apron strings. She had acquiesced readily enough to Anne's engagement to

Gerald two years before, but when it came down to setting the date for the big event, she had balked time and time again.

Lili had heard plenty of tears and remonstrances from her closest companion regarding this, and she was glad that things had finally been settled at last. Still, her happiness on behalf of her friend could not help but be colored by the misery that she felt lurking within her soul, like something ancient and hidden in the cellar.

Her aunt, with the curious perception that had always taken Lili by surprise regardless of how often she exercised the ability, appeared at her side during the festivities after the ceremony.

"A beautiful occasion, isn't it," Hester Melville murmured.

Lili lifted her chin and turned her face away, hoping to conceal her expression from her aunt – though she knew it was pointless to attempt. Aunt Hester knew how she felt. She always knew.

"It is," she said, filling her voice with a determined attempt at sheer joy. "Anne is the most beautiful bride I've ever seen."

"Mm, indeed. And you've had plenty of opportunities to compare, my dear."

Lili bit her lower lip. Goodness, how was it that Aunt Hester could always see straight through her to her secret thoughts below the surface. For, of course, she had just been thinking of the fact that today made eight weddings – eight -- which she had attended over the past year. Every single last one of her childhood friends was married off and settled now; Agnes Birstock had only just last week announced the impending arrival of her first child. And here she was, Liliana Elison, an orphan with only her kind, keen-minded aunt for family, all alone otherwise. Not only did she not have a husband, but she also didn't even have a beau – or anything even close to one.

Just as she opened her mouth, ready to bemoan her situation aloud (since Aunt Hester seemed to know it anyway, she might as well relieve her feelings by complaining), her aunt smiled swiftly and said, "Of course, you might have been the most beautiful bride of all – if you'd had a mind to."

Lili closed her mouth with a snap, turning wide eyes on her aunt, who simply smiled gently at her. After a moment of gathering her thoughts, she managed, "Aunt Hester, you know how I feel about…"

"I know, my dear. Didn't I sit beside you all those nights after it first happened, holding your hand, and drying your tears?"

"Yes, but…" Lili bit her lip again, struggling with her desire to open up about the pain that seemed to follow her around everywhere she went, but knowing that her aunt had heard every word a dozen times and more. "It's only that I feel as though I'm – a widow, Aunt Hester, rather than a girl who may one day be a bride."

"Oh, my dear." Hester sighed and put an arm around her niece, drawing her into a fond embrace. Together, they watched the dancing couples as they whirled about the floor. "I know that's how you feel – but it isn't the truth of the matter, and you know it. It's been over two years since poor Peter…" She trailed off, seeing the tensing in Lili's expression. Lili could feel her throat tighten at the very mention of his name. "And you never were married, my dear," Hester went on, her voice lower than before. "You were only his intended, never his wife."

Lili turned to face out at the dancing floor once more, her eyes growing damp.

"Aunt Hester, you know as well as I do that it isn't only marriage that creates a bond between a man and a woman. Love often comes well before the exchange of vows."

"I know. I know. It's only that I hate to see you tie your happiness to a single man – a man who has left this world behind for his eternal rest, and who can no longer do anything to ensure your happiness. You're only twenty-four years old, my dear one, and you have your whole future ahead of you."

Lili caught her breath.

"A future without Peter," she said. "Without the only man I've ever loved."

"I know, dear," Aunt Hester said, with a note in her voice that suggested she was holding back some things she would have dearly loved to speak out, "but he's only that because you've refused to look at anyone else. Why, I'm certain that Mr. Graham would have courted you if you'd given him the slightest encouragement."

"Matthew Graham? Why, he's just a silly boy."

"And Adelaide's son was over the moon for you."

"Abel Thompkins would be over the moon for any girl who looked his way twice."

"Mr. John Partridge, then," said Aunt Hester, folding her arms with a show of irritation – though there was a hint of amusement in her voice at the same time. "What have you to say against a fine, upstanding man like that?"

"John Partridge is a fine, upstanding man," Lili agreed, her voice softening. John had been a friend of the family for as long as she could remember; he was a good fifteen years older than she and had laid his first beloved wife to rest when Lili was still a child. Since then, he had been the kindest, most staunch ally to Lili and her aunt that they could have hoped for, stepping in with generosity when times were scarce, always ensuring that they had what they needed. He was the closest thing to a benefactor that she had ever known, and extremely handsome to boot. She pulled herself out of her idyll and said firmly, "But he's not Peter.

Besides, he's courting Susan Richie now, and you know Sue won't let her claws out of him for a moment."

"Indeed," said Aunt Hester, eyeing her niece for a moment. "My dear, you know that I adore you, and think that you are everything good in the world."

Lili blushed faintly.

"Far from it, Aunt Hester – as you well know – but thank you. On occasions such as these, it soothes my soul to hear a kind word."

Aunt Hester had not quite finished. Her tone gentling as she spoke, she went on, "But I must speak my mind, because I am your only guardian. My dear Lili, I'm afraid you're in grave danger of becoming a bitter old lady."

Lili turned to stare at her.

"Aunt Hester."

"Yes, I'm afraid it's true. I've noticed the tendency for some time now, my dear, but my love for you compels me now to no longer overlook it but to speak up. I know that you were very fond of Peter, Lili – but the truth is that you were never so devoted to him until after he succumbed to terrible illness, and I very much fear that your dedication stems from guilt, rather than a case of true love."

"Aunt Hester."

"Furthermore, I don't believe that you would be so very upset by the weddings of your closest childhood friends, were it not for the fact that you clearly feel as though you have missed out. What could have caused you to turn down the offers and attention of good, honorable men – men whom you have been friends with for years, and whom you never saw fault with until they set their caps for you? Why, I hesitate to condemn you all at once, my dear, but I fear it's nothing less than sheer stubbornness."

"Aunt – Aunt Hester."

"It isn't as though you don't come by it honestly," Hester went on thoughtfully. "My dear sister was extremely stubborn herself, and certainly had a tendency toward the romantic – and when she could not have the romantically happy, she chose the romantically tragic instead. Can such a thing be handed down in the bloodline, I wonder? But I hardly suffer with such thoughts myself..."

"Aunt Hester." This time, Lili reached out and grasped her aunt by the elbow. "Can we speak in private, please?" she whispered. "I feel as though everyone in the room is staring at us."

Her aunt chuckled.

"Yes – that sounds rather like something your mother would have said, too. Of course, my dear. Come with me." She tucked Lili's arm through hers and led her to the big double doors at the front of the hall. The wedding reception was being held in one of the larger gathering places in their neighborhood of Boston; though Anne Brown was just as poor as Lili and her aunt had always been, Gerald Hapstay was the only son and heir of Hapstay Manufacturing, one of the largest manufacturing concerns in all of Massachusetts. That being the case, there was plenty of room in the hall, even though half of Boston had turned out to see Gerald and Anne get married; there was little fear of their conversation being overheard. Still, it soothed Lili's emotions somewhat to be led out into the bright sunshine of late spring, and she took a deep breath before turning to her aunt.

"I don't see how you can say such things…"

"But, of course you do, Lili," Aunt Hester said without waiting for her to finish. "And what's more, you know in your heart that I'm perfectly right."

"I certainly do not. I loved Peter Allbright, Aunt Hester – I loved him with every breath in my being."

"Well, perhaps you did," said her aunt with a practical sigh. "But I simply cannot allow you to fritter away your life clinging to his memory. If you won't admit to it and move on yourself, I shall find myself forced to take drastic measures."

Lili stared at her aunt in consternation.

"What on earth do you mean by that, Aunt Hester?"

"I mean, my dear, that I've taken it upon myself to have a conversation with an old friend of mine – Alice Randall.

She's a widow now, you know, with a business mind as sharp as they come. Just last year, she took over a thriving concern down on Placer Street – a matrimonial agency."

"Aunt Hester."

"Goodness," said her aunt mildly. "If you're in fear that I'm so old I'll forget my own name, you needn't be. Reminding me of it every moment or so isn't necessary."

Lili shook her head. She could scarcely believe what her aunt was implying – and said as much.

"Well, you must make up your mind to believe it," said her aunt briskly. "As a matter of fact, Alice has already discovered the perfect match for you – a distinguished gentleman who runs his family's ranch, in a little town in Missouri."

"Missouri."

"Yes, dear, Missouri. Alice has heard very good things about him – from what she's told me, he sounds a great deal like our old friend John Partridge. At any rate, my dear, the truth is that I'm getting on in years – I was much older than your mother, you know – and after that terrible bout of sickness last winter, Adam has asked me to move out to Prestonville and live with him. Do you remember visiting Adam and his wife in Prestonville?"

"Yes, of course," said Lili, somewhat distracted by this. Her cousin was a good decade older than her, a staid and stable man who seemed to have none of his mother's insight, let alone her intelligence. Oh, dear, had she just thought such a scornful thing about her cousin, who was one of the least objectionable people she'd ever met? Perhaps her aunt was right. Perhaps she was turning into a bitter old lady.

But she was only twenty-four. She couldn't stand for such a thing.

"I remember," said Hester, "that you didn't think much of Prestonville. It's very small, of course, nothing like Boston. And there are precious few young men who might have a hope of capturing your fancy. You're welcome to come along with me, of course, my dear, but – don't you think that Missouri sounds like a much more attractive option?"

Slowly, Lili turned to face her aunt, eyes fixed on hers.

"You've already made up your mind about this, haven't you?" she said. "You've arranged for me to have somewhere to go, and to be married to this – this ranch owner in the middle of nowhere. Does it matter much what I say to the contrary? You'll brook no argument."

Her aunt smiled and chucked her under the chin.

"Well, there you have it," she said cheerfully. "I suppose I do show some traits of stubbornness after all. It must run in the family. Quite seriously, Liliana, I have indeed been considering this for some time. You may not think that I know what's best for you – and perhaps I don't. Who knows what the good Lord might have in store for you? But I do know one thing – his plan does not involve the prettiest, smartest, sweetest girl in all of Massachusetts spending her days alone, pining over a man because she feels guilty that she didn't love him quite enough."

Lili pressed her lips together.

"I did love him," she insisted. "I did. He was the love of my life, Aunt Hester, and nothing you can say will convince me otherwise."

"All right, then, my dear, I won't try and convince you. But really, Lili – whoever told you that you only ever have one chance at love?" She put a hand on Lili's shoulder and smiled at her tenderly. "You're too young to allow your heart to wear widow's weeds. Go to Missouri, my dearest girl. Go to Missouri, and marry, and be happy."

Lili took in a long breath and let it out in a deep sigh.

"I'll go to Missouri," she said. "I hardly think I have any other choice. But as for the rest – well, I cannot promise either to marry or to be happy. Not even to please you, Aunt Hester, though I do love you very much."

Again, Hester tipped Lili's chin up with her fingertips, smiling down at her.

"That's my girl," she said, warmly.

CHAPTER 2

On the first day of July, Liliana Elison sat with her nose almost pressed up against the glass window of the train and caught her first sight of her new hometown – Culver's Creek, Missouri.

She told herself that she was quite disappointed. The train station was tiny, with only one little wooden platform. The town that they had rolled through before reaching it was scarcely more than a neighborhood, in her opinion; she had grown up in Boston and knew little other than streets after streets, tall buildings and cobbled roads, busy passersby hurrying from one place to the next. This, though – Culver's Creek was anything but "busy." She saw a handful of people, no more. Perhaps that was only to be expected, for it wasn't as though there were many places for them to be going to.

As much as she told herself that this was a grave disappointment, she had to admit to herself that she was secretly rather charmed by the little town. Everything was neatly whitewashed, all the buildings constructed alike of hand-split boards. There was a wooden sidewalk running along both sides of the street, to keep the townsfolk out of the mud during the rainy weather. A necessity, evidently, for there were no cobbles to be seen and all four of the main streets were made of hard-packed dirt – or, rather, dust. A small, hot breeze kicked up as she stepped out of the train, and a dust devil swirled in the distance.

As small as the town evidently was, she was surprised that so many seemed to be disembarking here – and that so many seemed to be ready to meet all who were arriving. Perhaps it was simply a stopover for them, she thought, but no – several of her erstwhile companions rushed forward, calling gladly to others on the small, crowded platform. She stepped aside, clutching the handles of her large carpetbag, feeling suddenly rather resentful of the circumstances that had led her to be here at all. Why on earth had Aunt Hester made such a decision for her? In her fretfulness, she chose to overlook her own part in the case. Why, what she wouldn't give to be back home again right this minute.

Only there was no going back, she reminded herself sternly. Her aunt was even now packing up the last of her boxes, tidying up the empty house. Soon she would be on her way to Prestonville to meet Adam and his wife, Sarah, who would welcome her with open arms and would be secretly rather glad that Lili was not in tow.

Her aunt's premonition was not yet set to rest. Now Lili felt very bitter, indeed.

Unconsciously, she scowled as she looked about the platform, wondering who this rancher might be who was meant to meet her. There were only a few people left on the platform now, most of them having already gone on their way. At the far end of the platform, near the stairs, she saw a figure with his face half turned away.

His profile caught at her like a grasping hand, and she felt her heart leap in her chest. There was something so dark and familiar in it, the noble brow, the strong, definite nose and chin, the outline of well-cut lips…

"Peter."

The name escaped her before she could stop herself. On any other train platform in any other station in the world, there would have been too much noise for her voice to be heard. Here in Culver's Creek, Missouri, she had no such luck. The few remaining people on the platform turned to face her – including the gentleman who had caused her outcry to begin with.

He turned his head, first, his eyes seeking her out. Her heart sank, for of course it was not Peter – Peter was no longer part of this world but had left her behind for a greater rest than any he'd ever had on earth. It wasn't Peter, but it was a good-looking stranger who bore some strong resemblance to the man she had once been engaged to, the man she had loved. He was tall, with rather slim, narrow shoulders; he carried himself with an air of wariness, rather than confidence, as though unsure what might happen but determined to be ready for it. His back was very straight, his shoulders very square. His narrow face with its well-defined features was almost too full of character for handsomeness – but he managed it, all the same. She felt her heart leap again, though for quite a different reason this time.

He was coming toward her, a look of determination in his eye.

Trailing along behind him was an older woman; Lili judged her to be somewhere in her sixties, though she was quite well-preserved. Her hair was long and fair, piled high in an artfully arranged style on her head; she was a good two feet shorter than the man, but as soon as he stopped in front of Lili, she stepped around him as though he were a child and could not be trusted to speak for himself.

"Miss Elison? Miss Liliana Elison?"

Lili gathered herself; it was more difficult to do so than she would have expected, for the tall, handsome stranger was looking down at her with a quizzical expression in his black eyes.

"Er, yes," she said. "I'm Lili Elison."

The older woman gave a firm nod.

"I thought you must be," she said. "It's rare enough that we see an unfamiliar face around here in Culver's Creek, and just about a once in a lifetime occurrence for it to be a young woman, all on her own. She stuck out a hand, and when Lili went to shake it, she took her bag from her and handed it to the man at her side. "We're awful glad that you could make it. I'm Liza, Liza Morris. This here is my nephew, Orpheus Miller. Well, I reckon you know the name about as well as your own, by now – he's to be your husband."

Lili's throat felt suddenly dry. Though she had certainly taken note of the tall stranger – his handsomeness, his resemblance to Peter – the thought had never crossed her mind that he might be her intended groom. Now, with this new thought overtaking everything else, she looked back up at him with a startled curiosity. Why, he was – old. No, not old, she amended to herself hastily; but certainly not young, either. He wore a hat, but she could see that he was going gray at the temples. His dark eyes were lively, but there were fine lines, crow's feet, around them; his well-cut lips were thin, though they suggested a former fullness in his youth. He must be well over a decade older than she was herself – and at the thought, she suddenly realized why Aunt Hester had told her that this Orpheus Miller put her in mind of their old friend, John Partridge. He was older, distinguished, a gentleman – and she felt suddenly very young and silly, standing next to him.

The only logical reaction to being made to feel young and silly, even accidentally, was resentment, and she felt the feeling flood through her in spades. She drew herself up and lifted her chin.

"How very pleasant to meet you, Mr. Miller," she said formally. He shifted her bag to his left hand and extended his right; she put her own hand into it and felt very small indeed. His long fingers closed around hers and he bent down a little, eyes searching through her as though he could not quite believe who she was.

Suddenly, he said, "Why did you call me Peter?"

Taken aback, and fighting a blush of embarrassment, Lili said, "I didn't call you Peter."

"No?" He tilted his head curiously. "I could have sworn…"

"I – I thought I saw someone who looked familiar, someone that I knew back in Boston," she managed, striving to mitigate her little white lie with something closer to the truth.

"Someone named Peter?" Orpheus Miller suggested.

"Yes." The blush was growing deeper by the second. Why, oh, why did he have to look at her like that?

"A friend of yours?"

She opened her mouth to reply, then hesitated. The last thing she wanted to have to do was explain about her long-lost love, whom she had lost to such a terrible illness, and whom she had loved so deeply that she resented the very fact that she was here, talking to a man who reminded her so starkly of him.

"A – cousin," she said. "I mean – a brother. I mean – my cousin's brother."

One dark eyebrow raised, but he kept his tone polite.

"I believe – and I may well be wrong, Miss Elison – but I believe that your cousin's brother would also be...your cousin."

"Half-brother," she said hurriedly. "My cousin's half-brother. We're scarcely related at all, really, and I haven't seen him for years. I suppose that explains why I thought I saw him. My memory was playing tricks on me, or my eyes."

"Have you any reason to suspect that your half-cousin Peter might be here in Culver's Creek, Missouri?"

She was not so flustered that she couldn't hear and understand the gentle sarcasm in his voice. Bristling a little, she narrowed her eyes at him.

"I'm sure I haven't the faintest idea where he's got to," she said. "As I said, it's been many years. He might as well be here in Culver's Creek as anywhere else, I suppose."

To her shock, a wide, white grin spread over Orpheus Miller's face, and suddenly he became very attractive indeed. His smile was nothing like Peter's.

"That's what I always reckon," he said. "Might as well be here as anywhere else. Well, Miss Elison, we're glad to have you." He swept one arm out in an inviting gesture. "And now, if you'd like, Aunt Liza and I'll take you on home."

Not for the first time, Lili had the feeling that she had little say in the matter. Pressing her lips together, she nodded and followed along behind Orpheus Miller and his aunt.

Liza Morris, for her part, was not the sort of woman to allow an uncomfortable silence to grow and spread. As they walked toward the cart that was waiting for them just around the corner, she filled Lili in with the sights and stories of Culver's Creek. There were more than Lili would have expected, from the size of the town. Here on this corner, Orpheus's father, Patrick, had saved a little girl from being run over by a runaway mule. There on the next block was the mercantile, which was where everyone in town gathered in the winter, to sit around Mr. Knott's fireplace and tell tall tales until the springtime came again. There was the inn, where once the uncle of the President of the United States, one Sardis Birchard, had stayed when he was young.

"Has your family always lived here, then?" Lili asked, turning to Orpheus. She sat between him and his aunt in the driver's box of the cart; the back was full of her things, as well as several packages. Evidently, they had taken the opportunity to do some shopping and errands while in town. The ranch house, Liza mentioned early on in the storytelling, was a good twenty minutes away from town, when the horses weren't too tired.

"Just about," Orpheus Miller answered with a nod. "My great-grandfather came over from England when he was a boy, and within a few years of that, he'd made his way here. He was handed forty acres to begin with, to strike his claim, and by the time he married, he had a hundred and forty. He was a sharp fellow, my great granddad."

"Ever since then," Liza took up the story, "the Millers have been a mainstay of Culver's Creek. Why, my great-aunt Alonie Miller married one of the Culvers. So, you can see, Miss Elison, we're a well-established family. Even those of us who leave always end up finding our way back home..." She smiled, though there was a hint of something like embarrassment in her expression.

"Just like you did, Liza," said Orpheus with a grin.

Liza nodded, and her next words were directed to Lili again. "I married a fellow out in Boston, when I was little more than a girl – too young to know how hard it would be to leave my sister and my parents behind. That's how I came to write the letter to the matrimonial agency there, you see. My husband's family is still there, and my son has been living there for the past few years, as well. My sister-in-law found him a position as an office boy to a lawyer there – a very well-to-do man, so I'm led to believe, and now he's agreed to send Charles to school so he may be a lawyer too."

The mention of her hometown filled Lili with a brief sensation of yearning – how she longed to close her eyes and find herself magically transported back there. Forcing the feeling to heel, she said, "I don't know many lawyers in Boston. Except, of course, for Mr. John Partridge. He's an old friend of the family, and a very great man."

Orpheus Miller and Liza Morris exchanged glances, and then they both chuckled; there was an unmissable note of disbelief in Liza's laugh.

"Well, I'll be." she declared. "If that isn't just the name of the fellow Charles is working for. Mr. Partridge, yes, that's it. I'd never forget a name like that, even if he hadn't been so kind to my boy. Well, Charles is delighted to be working with him, and if you're a friend of Mr. Partridge, then I'm certain we'll all get along just fine." She gave Lili a little nudge with her elbow and beamed at her. Lili smiled back, even as she felt a faint feeling of doubt creep over her.

After all, it was all well and good to find that they had an acquaintance in common – though she was beginning to regret more than ever that she had turned John Partridge's attentions down – but there was so much about this situation that she hadn't been aware of before she'd agreed to it. Orpheus Miller's age, for one thing – and surely a man so close to forty must have been married before? She wasn't sure how she felt about marrying a widower. Or suppose he was even – divorced? She'd never met a divorced man before, but she knew that they existed.

On top of that, why was it that his aunt had been the one to write to the matrimonial agency? Suddenly, this seemed rather insulting to her – even suspicious. Shouldn't he have written on his own behalf if he wanted to be married? Or did he? Perhaps he was no more interested in matrimony than she was herself – but if that was the case, why was he standing for it? And what was wrong with her, that he would turn up his nose at the idea of marrying her? She felt suddenly quite betrayed by him – but in the very next moment, she had to laugh at herself. After all, she couldn't very well hold it against him if he was only going along with this to humor his aunt. Hadn't she done the very same thing? And as far as not writing to the agency himself, why, she was equally as guilty of that.

Perhaps they had more in common than met the eye.

She snuck a glance at him sideways, marveling yet again at how much he reminded her of Peter. He was so very handsome, she could not quite believe it – and yet, not handsome in the same way as any other man she'd ever met. He was distinguished, that was it, and quite different. She thought of the photograph of Peter pressed in the front cover of her diary and blushed suddenly. Yes, they had some things in common, but how could she have ever mistaken Orpheus Miller for Peter Allbright?

He seemed to sense her regard, but he didn't turn to look at her. Instead, she saw his dark eyes roll toward her as he looked at her out of the corner of them, and his mouth turned upwards in a smile. She felt suddenly as though the two of them were sharing a secret, a secret buried so very deep that she didn't quite know it herself, and yet she was the bearer of it, along with him. She wanted to smile – and so she did.

In almost the same instant, she felt a stab of guilt like the strike of a dagger – guilt that she was smiling at this handsome man, when Peter Allbright was cold and dead.

She turned her head away from him and faced forward with determination. She sensed him looking at her, now, his head turned toward her, but she would not look back.

He might remind her of Peter, but that meant nothing. Less than nothing. He was a stranger, and she was only here to please her aunt.

And that, she thought firmly, was all.

CHAPTER 3

Orph Miller was only half-asleep, but the sound of the knock on the door startled him out of his stupor. He sat up in his chair and rubbed his face with both hands as his aunt came into the room, bearing a tray on her arm. She gave him a sympathetic smile and turned her attention to the slight figure in the bed.

Rose Miller was still sleeping, but at her younger sister's light touch, her eyes fluttered open. She took in a deep breath, with that by-now-familiar gasp as though it pained her – a sound which pained Orph in turn. He leaned forward, elbows on his knees, and gave her a hopeful smile.

For a moment, Rose's lips moved soundlessly. Then she managed to find her voice.

"Good morning – Liza – and my boy…"

Orph reached over and took his mother's frail hand as Liza set the tray down beside her. Together, they helped Rose to sit up, propping her up against the headboard with pillows.

"You didn't fall asleep in here last night again, did you?" Liza said.

Orph shook his head. "Woke up about four o'clock this morning and couldn't get back to sleep. Checked in on Ma and she was awake, so I sat down to talk with her for a bit. I guess we both drifted off after that."

Liza chuckled.

"Nothing soothes a worried mind like listening to you talk, I guess, Orph. Did you tell her about Miss Elison?"

Rose turned her head from one to the other, raising a thin, pale eyebrow.

"Miss Elison?" she murmured.

Orph sat down again beside her.

"I figured we'd wait until this morning to talk about it," he said. "Didn't want you to get all excited. You remember, Ma, that Aunt Liza wrote to the matrimonial agency over in Boston." His mother nodded. A faint gleam was coming into her eye, a sparkle that Orph was glad to see. Ever since his mother had begun to slowly progress toward her eternal rest, it had broken his heart to see the way her joy in life, her vitality, was being stripped away from her a little more every week. If nothing else, he thought, Miss Elison's presence was a boon to Rose's interest in life, for she had no strength to muster much enthusiasm for anything else.

"Well, the young lady arrived yesterday. Very young, as a matter of fact," he added, shooting Liza a sharp glance. "I'd figured you might tell the agency that I was no spring chicken, and they'd set me up with someone more my own age, but she's hardly more than a girl."

"Miss Elison is not a child," said Liza, with dignity. "And I did, in fact, inform the agency that you were near forty."

Orph winced a little.

"Thirty-eight," he said. "Don't call me an old man just yet."

"Thirty-eight, and with the strength and vigor of a man ten years younger," said his aunt, smiling at his vanity and rumpling his hair as though he were still a boy. "I'm sixty myself, Orph – you can't imagine that I would think of forty as old."

"Still," said Orph. "Let's not rush these things, eh? Anyway, she's here safe and sound," he said, returning his attention to his mother. "And she seems quite…" He hesitated, looking for the word. "Capable," he said at last, and flushed faintly, for it wasn't the word he wanted to use at all.

"More than that." said his aunt defensively. "She's sweet, Rose, but she knows her own mind. I think we'll all get along perfectly well. Besides, she knows the lawyer that Charles is employed by, the one who's sending him to school – old friend of the family, she says."

Rose nodded, her thin lips curving in a tired smile.

"Good," she said. "I'm glad." She took hold of Orph's hand once more, and squeezed it as tightly as she could. It was a faint echo of a strong woman's grasp. He smiled down at her. Even the ten years he'd spent away from home in the army had not changed how his mother felt about her boy; he was the only son of the Miller family, and the only remnant of the long and loving relationship she'd had with her husband. She had never complained about his service or told him how she wished he would come home and settle down; it wasn't until after his father's death and Orph's honorable discharge that she even voiced her heart's desire for her son to marry and have children. Orph had already been thirty-five by that point, and all his childhood peers were well settled with growing families.

There were precious few unmarried women in the entire county, and it wasn't until his aunt began to speak about the possibility of a mail order bride that he even thought of marriage as a possibility. Still, he'd held off – "balked" was the word his aunt had used, repeatedly – until he understood how dearly his mother wanted grandchildren.

Even then, he couldn't bring himself to write the letter himself. Rose Miller was bedridden and growing sicker by the day when her younger sister took it upon herself to write to the agency – for the good of everyone involved, she had said firmly.

And Orph knew in his heart that it was the right thing to do.

It wasn't as though he hadn't planned to marry. He supposed that just about every fellow wanted a wife and children. He was no different from the rest – just a little older, was all. And now that he was settled down in Culver's Creek again, in charge of the ranch he'd grown up on, he found himself growing a little lonely. It would be nice to have someone to talk to – and someone to hold him, to understand his feelings, when his ma slipped away from her painful life at last and went to her final rest.

He could only hope that she would live to see the first of her grandchildren – if he married Miss Elison at all.

He was glad that neither his mother nor his aunt pressured him to tell them how he felt on the subject. The truth was, he could not make up his mind. On the one hand, Liliana Elison was nearly fifteen years younger than he was. He knew, too, that it was her own aunt who had applied on the agency and made their match on her behalf; he couldn't hold that against her, of course, as he had done precisely the same thing. But it gave a fellow insight into the inner workings of a young woman's mind, didn't it, when he knew that she was not here entirely by choice?

And then there was the matter of this "Peter," whom she said she thought she recognized.

He was still pretty sure that she had thought he, Orph Miller, was this Peter. And her story about it being her cousin – or her brother's cousin – or her cousin's brother – or any other relative – was so patently false that he'd only kept himself from laughing by a strong, concerted effort. No doubt about it, there was something there that she was hiding. Some fellow, more specifically, and he couldn't help but think that there must have been some romantic attachment.

After all, she was a beautiful, lively young woman.

And that was the other side of the coin – he was a normal, red-blooded man, despite of (or perhaps because of) his bachelorhood at his age, and he could not deny the fact that he found Liliana Elison to be incredibly attractive.

She was a bit stand-offish, that was true. He supposed it was only natural, given the circumstances. And in the little they had spoken the previous night, before she'd pled exhaustion and gone to bed early, he had found glimpses and glimmers of a healthy sense of humor, an honesty, and a straightforwardness that he found just as appealing as her physical beauty. Yes, he knew by the faltering of his heart that he could very easily fall in love with this young woman – and yet, he was conscious of the need to hold himself back.

He wasn't what she had expected, of that, he was sure.

Suppose she decided that she wanted to marry someone else? Someone closer to her age, perhaps – or this "Peter"?

He had lapsed into deep thought, only half listening to his aunt tell his mother all about their first meeting with Miss Elison. He came back to himself to hear her say, cheerfully, "But then, I needn't tell you everything, when you can ask her yourself. Come in, Miss Elison, come in. Did you rest well?"

With a shy smile, Lilian Elison did as she was bid. Her blue eyes darted around the room, first to the slight figure in the bed, then to Liza, and finally to Orph. As their eyes met, she looked away hastily, and a blush darkened her cheeks.

"Good morning," she said. "I hope I'm not intruding."

"Not at all," said Liza. "In fact, I was just about to go back downstairs to the kitchen and ask you to come up. It's time you met my sister, Rose. She is Orph's mother."

To be introduced in such a manner would be a challenge for anyone, Orph thought. He knew just what his mother looked like; he did not fool himself. She was so frail she was little more than skin and bones, little more than a slight rise under the counterpane. Speaking was obviously painful for her, and she could not feed herself; Liza sat close, helping her to sip her tea. Were it not for the fire of life and interest that burned in Rose's eyes, anyone would have thought that she was on death's doorstep – and not everyone could see that burning flame.

He watched Liliana Elison with guarded curiosity, waiting to see what she did.

33

He saw her take a deep breath, and then she stepped forward. Her smile spread, widened, and became more genuine. She reached out and laid a hand on Rose's frail palm, upturned on the bedspread, and then got to her knees beside the bed to hold it.

"I'm very pleased to meet you, Mrs. Miller," she said, her voice soft. "Your family has shown me such hospitality, and I'm grateful for it. Thank you for opening your home to a stranger from far away."

Orph felt his heart rise into his throat as he saw his mother begin to smile. She lifted a fragile hand and cupped Miss Elison's chin.

"How very sweet you are," she whispered. "I'm so very glad that you are here, my dear. I think we will all get along very well."

Orph had to look away, fighting the sudden pricking of tears at the back of his eyes. As uncertain as he was about Liliana Elison, he could not help but feel a sudden surge of gratitude toward her. No matter what came next, he would always feel that same way: grateful for the smile she had brought to his mother's face, and for the tone he heard in her voice – calm, and peace, and, for the first time in a very long time, hope.

CHAPTER 4

The ranch outside of Culver's Creek was capacious, to say the least – the house was enormous, far larger than any she had ever lived in, either with her impoverished parents or her equally poor aunt. Given free range to explore, she spent a few days wandering through it.

Upon her questioning, Liza Morris had explained the size of it with a rueful smile.

"Our Grandfather Miller had it built," she said. "He had his eye set on a young woman in town and wanted to provide her with the prettiest and biggest house to call home. I reckon he thought they'd have a full baker's dozen of children, too, from the size of it. Well, things didn't turn out quite like he thought. They had three – one died in infancy, and the other two certainly couldn't fill up the empty space. Even when they had children of their own, for Orph's father was an only child and so is Orph himself, as you know. My husband and I came to live with my sister after she married Patrick, but all we managed was Charles, our son. It's a little livelier when Charles comes home to visit, but it's certainly not what Grandfather Miller envisioned, I bet."

"May I ask why there were so few children?" Lili ventured. It could be a sore subject, she knew, and she was reluctant to give offense, despite her curiosity. Liza had been very kind to her since her arrival.

Liza gave a little shrug.

"It's a hard life here," she said. "Not uncommon for wives to lose their little ones before they're even born." She turned her head away, and Lili bit her lip, regretting that she had asked so sensitive a question. She put her hand on Liza's arm.

"I'm sorry, I didn't mean to bring you any painful memories."

Liza shook her head and managed a smile.

"All behind me now," she said. "I'm old enough to be a grandmother, whenever Charles makes up his mind to settle down. He's a few years older than you are – Bill and I had him later in our lives. I'd practically given up on having any children at all. He was our miracle boy." She smiled a bit more warmly now. "And things are better now than they were when I was younger. Why, by the time you and

Orpheus decide to have children, I reckon you'll have a passel of 'em before you know it."

Lili felt her heart jump a little in her chest. Married to Orpheus Miller – and the mother of his children. Oh, yes, that was what she had signed up for in agreeing to come here, but – somehow, the casual way in which Liza Morris was encouraging her made her feel rather strange. Did she want to be a mother? Surely. She'd always wanted to have children, though she had made up her mind to accept the fact that she never would, after Peter's passing. Now, the possibility of it loomed back up over her, more of a certainty than ever. Someday soon, she would stand beside Orpheus Miller in the little chapel in town, and say her vows, and be bound forever.

It gave her a little shiver – though not an entirely unpleasant one.

If that was the case, she thought decisively, then she would certainly have to spend more time with him and get to know him better.

Thus far, in the nearly a week since her arrival in town, they'd had precious few conversations together. Oh, he was polite and mannerly at meals, and always asked courteously how she was and whether she was in need of anything. But he spent most of his time outdoors, working away on the ranch. A responsible place to be, she supposed, but still – if he really did want to marry her, wouldn't he take the time to seek out her friendship?

Then again...perhaps he didn't really want to marry her at all. She could not discount such an idea until it was proven otherwise. After all, he, too, had relied upon a family member to correspond with the matrimonial agency.

At the very least, he could stop being quite so aloof and polite. She'd seen definite hints of a sense of humor during their first meeting – a sense of humor that she found appealing, despite herself. And she did like his obvious care for his invalid mother, who reminded her strongly of her own mother before she passed away. It was touching, to say the least. It got to her heart to see him sitting at her bedside, holding her hand – it made her feel rather warm and soft inside...

Well, perhaps neither of them truly wanted to be married. But if he wasn't going to take the necessary time to find out for certain, she would have to take charge.

It was in this spirit that she went in search of him one afternoon in mid-July, nearly two weeks after her arrival. He had not come in for the noon-time meal that day; Liza guessed that he was in the middle of some project or other that he simply got caught up in and forgot the time. Lili wrapped up a sandwich for him, poured lemonade into a cold flask, and then went in search of him, with determination in her step.

The Millers employed four ranch hands, and she had to ask each one before she was finally directed to the barn. It was stiflingly hot and still out, and she felt rather flushed and irritable as she stepped into the shade of the huge old structure. Still, he was nowhere in sight; she called for him, and after a moment he poked his head over the edge of the loft, his eyebrows furrowed in consternation.

"Miss Elison?"

They had discussed, in passing, the idea of referring to each other by their Christian names. The invitation had been exchanged, and yet he still forgot and reverted to "Miss Elison" at times, as though they were hardly more than acquaintances. It was a simple slip of the tongue – and a polite one – and yet, it simply reinforced for her the possibility that he wasn't keen on getting to know her at all, let alone marry her.

"Orpheus," she said firmly, feeling as though it was time to take the bull by the horns, "I've brought you a sandwich, as you didn't have the time to come in for lunch."

His silvery head disappeared for a moment, and here he came climbing swiftly down the ladder. She put a hand on her hip, raising her eyebrows as she waited for him; he gave her a sheepish smile.

"I'm sorry – Lili," he said. "Time just got away from me, that's all."

"Oh? I suppose you were working on something very important."

"Well, sure," he said, scratching the back of his neck. "There's always something needs doing on the ranch. I'm still getting the hang of running this place, even though it's been a few years. Reckon I'll get it eventually."

His slight smile, accompanying these words, was an invitation for her to soften and express her confidence in him. It was a very appealing smile. Perversely, it made her feel as though she wanted to pick a fight instead.

"However," she said, "none of your ranch hands seemed to know precisely what it was you were doing. Hank thought you might be re-roofing the chicken coop – you weren't. Tom suggested I check the corrals – you weren't there. Next, I was directed to the southern meadow – I didn't even know where that was, and by the time I found it, you had evidently escaped again, so I returned to ask Frederick, who thought he might have seen you headed for the barn, as the stables needed mucking out. And here you are, though not, I must note, doing any mucking."

Orph's smile turned somewhat nervous.

"Well, no," he admitted, "not doing any mucking. Matter of fact, I come out here just to sit and think, sometimes – and I felt the need to do just that this afternoon."

She widened her eyes at him.

"So you could just as easily have come in for lunch, and saved me all that traipsing around looking for you?"

He rubbed the back of his neck again, looking somewhat dubious.

"Well," he said, "I reckon I'm grateful that you did, but – I didn't ask you to, Lili, and…"

She set the basket down with a thump and folded her arms.

"I suppose not." she said. "But when I considered you missing your meal because, as I supposed, you were slaving away – well, what do you expect any thoughtful female to do?"

"It was awful thoughtful of you, for sure…"

"On top of that, it's been nearly two weeks since I arrived here, and you and I have hardly said a word to each other. I don't see how we're going to expect to be married when you're far too busy to spend any time getting to know me – I suppose that's a mark of the difference between a man and a woman, but I can't claim that I understand it."

Unexpectedly, his tone softened.

"I reckon that's my fault," he said, contritely. "I'm awful sorry, Lili. If I had any idea that you were thinking such a thing…"

"Oh, so it's my fault now, for not telling you precisely what I was thinking?"

"Now, I didn't say that, did I? I only meant it's as difficult for me to read your mind as it is for you to understand me. The difference between a man and a woman, you said. I reckon this is your first time gettin' to know a fellow well..."

"Oh, I understand you perfectly." she fired back, the words slipping out without her permission. "And as for it being my first time to grow close to a man – you haven't the faintest idea about my past."

His dark eyes narrowed slightly.

"Maybe so," he said, "maybe I'm ignorant. I'll tell you this, though – I'm Orph Miller. Not Peter your brother's cousin."

The words brought her up short, stopping her retort cold on her lips. The thought crossed her mind that she had come out here with the express purpose of spending time with him, to get to know him better. Surely arguing in this manner was an ineffective way to go about it – suddenly, she felt flushed with embarrassment. Why were they disagreeing with each other over such a small matter? She'd best leave well enough alone.

At the thought, she became abruptly determined to do just that.

"It doesn't matter much now," she said. "I've only come to tell you that I've – I've decided to go for a walk."

"A walk?"

"Yes."

"Where to?"

His question was gently put, despite his obvious irritation; still, she bristled under it.

"Into town, I suppose," she said. "Is there anywhere else to go? This isn't Boston."

"You're right, it isn't. And it's gettin' late in the afternoon, Lili."

"It would have been earlier if I hadn't spent so much time searching for you," she replied pertly. He frowned but didn't take her bait.

"There are parts of town that start to get less than savory around this time," he said, "especially as it's a Saturday night. Some of the menfolk can get a little rough around the edges."

She tossed her head.

"I'm sure they can't be any worse than they would have been in Boston," she said, mentally adding, though goodness knows my aunt always kept me far away from such things.

"I don't know about that," Orph said, frowning even more deeply now. "Men around here don't see pretty girls every day – and you're a stranger to the area, too. If you don't have someone with you to protect you…"

His comment, as casual as it was, made her heart leap briefly. Pretty – he called me pretty… Perversely, she lifted her chin proudly.

"I don't need protecting," she declared.

"It's scarier out there than you might think."

"I'm used to the big city. I can't imagine that anything Culver's Creek has to throw at me could be more dangerous than that."

"Maybe not, but there's no sense asking for trouble. You ought to let me come with you."

She pressed her lips together.

"I don't see why."

"For safety."

"I'll be perfectly safe."

"For mine, then," he said, giving her a grin, though she could see his eyes still betrayed his worry. "I never venture out this late in the day."

"Of course not – you're far too busy."

Suddenly, she realized that they were standing very close together. Somehow, without even registering the motion, they had taken step after step toward each other, and now they were practically nose to nose. The thought flitted across her mind and was gone – another inch or two, and he could lower his head just a little and kiss her…

Swallowing hard, she took a step back.

"I'm going for a walk," she said. "And I'll be just fine."

"That you will be," Orph said. His voice was a little unsteady; she wondered if he was gritting his teeth. It sounded an awful lot like it. "Because I'll be with you the whole way. It's too far to walk into town, anyhow, Lili. Let me saddle up the mare, and I'll take you."

And with this final display of stark logic, she could no longer argue. Still, it didn't keep her resentment from building. Why, did he think that she was incapable of taking care of herself? Her life had been far fuller of danger and excitement than his, if she had to guess. By his own admission, he'd grown up here in Culver's Creek, this little nothing town, whereas she had lived in the big city…

By the time he finished saddling the horse, she was fuming.

It didn't help that his grip on her waist, as he lifted her into the saddle, felt strangely comforting. Neither did it help that she was forced to hold tightly onto him around his waist as the mare moved into a smooth canter. He smelled of straw and leather and something she couldn't quite put her finger on – something both smoky and pure, like sunlight in the autumn.

She closed her eyes and held on tightly.

Before she knew it, they were in Culver's Creek. As they rode through, with the horse slowing to a gentle walk, she heard the friendly calls and halloos from those on the streets. It was, indeed, later in the day than she had thought; she would never have made it into town and back before dark, if she had insisted on walking. He stopped the mare at a corner near the mercantile and reached up to help her down to the solid ground. He seemed to hold onto her for just a split second longer than necessary.

"Now," he said, firmly, "it'll be dark soon, and there's no way out of that. My advice is to stay away from the saloon – the whole area of the saloon, in fact, 'cause there's no telling how early in the day some of those men started their Saturday drinking."

She narrowed her eyes at him.

"You never take a drink yourself, I suppose," she said.

"Not exactly never," he replied evenly. "In my younger years, I was known to frequent the saloon as often as the rest."

"Oh? And what happened, then?"

He rubbed his chin, eyeing her thoughtfully.

"I left home and joined the army," he said. "That's when I found out what real drinking meant. But that doesn't mean that the fellows here are never dangerous; there's been fistfights and shootings and plenty of cheating at poker, all the same."

She swallowed hard, feeling her stomach give a nervous quiver.

"All right, then," she said. "I promise not to get involved with men who cheat at poker."

He huffed out a short laugh and let her go at last, turning to the horse.

"Go to the left at the corner," he advised her, "and you'll save yourself a lot of trouble. Wait for me just a minute, and I'll walk with you. Lady here deserves a feedbag for coming into town so late in the day."

She hesitated, but only a moment. While his back was turned to her, she spun on her heel and hurried away. She stepped into the street to avoid alerting him with the sound of her footsteps on the wooden sidewalk; on the dusty street, she was nearly noiseless as she half-ran toward the corner. It was a ridiculous, childish urge, she knew, and yet she couldn't seem to stop herself. He made her feel very young, very small, very unworthy of his attention. Whether he did it on purpose or not did not matter; he had seemingly rejected her attempts to get to know him, and now she wasn't about to let him set the rules himself. If she wanted to walk on her own, she would, and she would go where she wanted.

She had rounded the corner and was well out of sight before he noticed that she was gone. She heard him give a startled shout, calling her name, and smiled to herself, hurrying on.

She had no real intention of going to the area of the saloon. It wasn't as though she wanted to seek out trouble. But as she stretched her legs, enjoying the feeling of being in civilization again – if one could call Culver's Creek "civilization" – she paid more attention to how she felt and less to her surroundings. She didn't even realize that she had come up abreast of the saloon until she was just past it and the double doors were swung open.

Four men came out – men who had clearly started drinking away their Saturday evening well before the evening started. There was a yell from inside the saloon – "And don't come back, if you know what's good for you. Get on home." – and the four men laughed. One of them called back a series of curses over his shoulder but fell into sniggering immediately afterwards. Lili, turning to face them, froze as one looked in her direction.

"Well, hey there."

Now all four of them were looking at her. She felt frozen, like a rabbit staring down a coyote. They weren't far from her, not more than a few feet. Hating the need to flee, she took a step back, and then another.

"Hold on, hold on," called one, and quick-stepped closer to her, abandoning his fellows. He held his hands out, palms down, to show his harmlessness, and smiled at her. He was quite handsome, she thought wildly, though his attractiveness was of a very different, more typical style than

Orpheus's unusual looks. "Don't be afraid, missy – we won't hurt you. Come on back here and talk to us. It's been a long time since I've seen a girl as pretty as you."

His words were sweet – almost sweet enough to cause her to lower her guard. She hesitated, and he stepped forward again and caught hold of her wrist. The suddenness of the movement took her by surprise, and she screamed.

An answering yell came from down the street. Suddenly, Orpheus Miller was in their midst, bowling aside the three other men to reach her. He caught hold of the fourth man's arm and twisted it, shoving him away from Lili. His face was dark with anger.

"Don't you touch the lady."

The fourth man's sweet smile turned into a sneer.

"Well, if it ain't the war hero. The cream of the crop. It's been a long time since we've seen you around here, Orph Miller."

Orph turned away from him, his eyes seeking out Lili's. She expected anger from him – fury, even – but there was nothing but concern.

"Are you all right, Lili?"

"I'm – I'm fine..." She took a deep breath and nodded. "He didn't hurt me, he just...took me by surprise, that's all. No harm done."

She managed a brave smile, hoping that Orph wouldn't perceive how desperately she wanted to cling to him, grateful that he had arrived to save her from...from whatever the other fellow had in mind.

He returned a faint smile to her.

"Reckon it's a little different from how things were in Boston," he said softly.

She bit her lip, nodding tremulously, but the four men behind him had heard his words and pricked up their ears.

"Boston, eh?" said one, leering at Lili. "That explains why we haven't seen a girl like her around here before – if she's specially imported."

"What's she doing all the way out here in Colorado?" asked the one who had put his hand on her arm. "Don't tell me she's here for you, Orph – now, that's not fair, is it?"

"Reckon his auntie asked Charlie to send her over," said another, grinning. "He's gettin' so old, they knew he'd never be able to hunt one down himself."

Lili's eyes met Orph's, and they stared at each other. His eyes were calm, though there was a banked fury deep within them, and she suddenly regretted deeply ever putting him in this position. He had been nothing but sweet to her, after all – he didn't deserve to have this abuse heaped on him for no reason.

"I'm sorry," she whispered.

Orph shook his head.

"Reckon we'd better get on home," he said. "Twilight's on its way."

"Oh, home, eh?" said the fourth man, his tone turning nasty. Orph held out a hand to Lili, and she took it, slipping her arm through his. Heads high, they started back past the four. "Hear that, fellows? Sounds like she's taken – or has been taken, anyhow. Reckon his ma knows that he's got a little chickadee staying in his room?"

Lili shot a swift glance at Orph. His jaw moved as his teeth clenched, but he said nothing.

"His ma don't know a thing," said another, laughing raucously. "She's so close to dyin', they're letting her plan her own funeral."

It was enough – no, it was far too much. Lili let go of Orph's arm and whirled around to face the four. The one nearest her was the one who had spoken. Clenching her hands at her sides, she lifted her leg, swung it back, and delivered a vicious kick to his shins. He howled and leapt, trying simultaneously to clutch his injured leg and run away from her, with the result that he went over sideways, knocking over the next man, too. They went down in a tangled spill of arms and legs, leaving their two companions to leap forward, swearing loudly.

Orph caught Lili by the shoulder and thrust her behind him. Almost in the same movement, his other fist, clenched and tight, lifted as he ducked the first blow thrown at him, and caught the other fellow on the chin. Lili longed to throw herself back into the fight, even if all she could do was kick; it wasn't right that Orph should have to defend her, when she was responsible for starting the fight to begin with. And hadn't he warned her that something like this might happen? Oh, yes, she was guilty, no doubt about it.

And still, there was something perfectly thrilling in watching Orpheus Miller fight for her honor. He fought like someone who had done so a hundred times before, and expected to do so a million times more before he was through. He fought like someone who knew so precisely what to do that it became something of an art. Her heart beating wildly in her chest, she clasped her hands in front of her, so tightly that her knuckles were white.

The commotion didn't go unnoticed by the denizens of the saloon.

"Here, now, what's going on out there?"

"It's Orph. Orph Miller."

"I just threw those four rascals out of here – someone call Sheriff Colley."

But the sheriff was already there, as though he'd been waiting for such a happening. He waded into the fray, and

Orph turned to nod his thanks to this reinforcement. His timing left much to be desired; with his attention divided, the fourth man took advantage of his opportunity, and caught Orph a crack to the jaw. The sound made Lili feel sick to her stomach.

Orph dropped like a stone at her feet.

CHAPTER 5

Dear Diary:

Oh, how I wish that Aunt Hester was here, so I could tell her everything. Of course, she probably knows precisely what's going on – and how I feel about it – and what I should do – because she always does, whether I tell her or not. Still, just because she can more than likely divine what I'm going through, it doesn't help me in the least. It neither relieves my feelings by allowing me to speak to her, nor gives me the benefit of her wisdom. (Though I suppose, if she was here to give me the benefit of her wisdom, it would simply irk me as it usually does...it's absence that makes the heart grow fonder, isn't it?)

In lieu of Aunt Hester, I suppose I should be grateful that I have this diary to put down my thoughts. I've looked back over the last several entries, covering the past few weeks of my life. It's almost startling to read my own words. Aunt Hester was afraid that I would turn into a bitter old lady if I didn't marry, but I'm finding quite a different tendency in my entries. A tendency that has taken me aback.

From the moment I met Orph Miller, I have been confused by him. Does he want to marry me, or doesn't he? Is he as distant and aloof as he seems, or is he instead a warm, vital, if rather shy man? He's nearly fifteen years older than I am, and yet he seems both much younger and yet again far older at times, depending on who he's speaking to and what he's speaking about. And yesterday, when he came to my rescue most valiantly – twice, I might add – I feel as though I saw another side of him entirely, a side I had not even suspected.

A side which, I'm terribly afraid, revealed a side of me, in turn, which was not expected, either.

I dreamed of him last night. At first, it was a frightening dream, for he was lying cold and still on the ground. Perhaps it had been another fight, in my dream, though for some strange reason I was certain that he was succumbing to the same illness that took poor Peter from his life at such a young age. No matter what the cause, there was no denying the effect on me: I called out in a panic and fell to my knees at his side, pressing his hand in mind, brushing his silvery hair back from his brow. And miraculously, he came to life again. His eyes opened and fixed on mine, and I felt the most amazing rush of warmth all through me, as though the sun had suddenly come out. He sat up and slipped his hands upwards, cupping my face in his, and then he...

I'm sitting here on the front porch. It's a few minutes later, and yet I'm still blushing madly. I cannot decide what to think about the dream. Only that I'm sure it was a manifestation of guilt – nothing more. Guilt that I led him into such a situation – for it was my fault that the men outside the saloon attacked us, after all, and there's no use in denying it – and guilt that I should think so fondly of Orph when I still see Peter in his features, when I glance his way... Oh, the more I get to know him, the more I see how different he is from Peter. But still, that first impression I had of him is very strong, and it seems nearly impossible to disentangle the two in my mind.

That's all it can be – entanglement. These dreams, these feelings, cannot be because of any attachment or attraction to Orph for his own sake. No, that I'm sure of. No matter what Aunt Hester would say.

Lili set her pencil down and leaned back in her chair, gazing ruminatively over the back yard. She cast her mind back to the day before – a day which had already been described in exhaustive detail in her treasured diary, and a day which would undoubtedly live on in her mind, clearly and distinctly, no matter how long she lived. It was horrible to see Orph crumple to her feet; he had been so still that for a wild, awful moment, she truly had believed that he'd been killed with that single blow. A dart of iron had entered her heart at that moment, and so she had written in her diary, wiping away reminiscent tears.

But he was only stunned, not killed. With the help of several of the townsfolk, she had gotten him to the doctor's house, where he was given time to recover. Half out of her mind with worry, she had nevertheless had the presence of mind to send a boy with word of their misadventure to the ranch house, not knowing when they might return. Orph had awoken not long after the blow and his transport to the home of Doctor Throwell; amid having his bruised and split knuckles bandaged, he had sat up and called for Lili at the top of his voice, looking around frantically.

The blow to his jaw had left him with a purpled and swollen chin, but nothing worse than that – for which she was grateful.

They had arrived home in the doctor's buggy, well after dark, to find Liza and Rose sitting up waiting for them.

The rest of the night had been near sleepless, and now, at the end of the long day that had followed, Lili found that exhaustion was creeping up on her once more. She closed her diary with a decisive clap, and forced herself up out of the chair. It was nearing supper time, which meant that it would be beginning to cool down before long. She would go in and help Liza with the meal, and then afterwards she could come back out to watch the sun go down.

With this intention at the forefront of her mind, she was baffled to find that her footsteps led in the opposite direction: toward the stairs.

She went up them noiselessly. At the edge of her hearing, she could just barely catch the murmur of a low voice – one she recognized, and one which tugged a little at her heart. There was that guilt again.

The door to Rose Miller's room stood ajar. She paused just outside it and looked in.

Rose – poor, sweet Rose. Her heart went out to her – lay on the bed, her head turned to the side. Her eyes were open, but only just; it was clear that she was drifting into rest. Still, her gaze and attention was fixed on her son. Orph sat close beside her, a book in his hand. He was reading to her – Dickens, Lili recognized – his voice low and quiet. His bandaged knuckles stood out stark white against the tanned brown of his skin, and she swallowed past the sudden lump in her throat. She could not bring herself to disturb them but stepped back away from the door without speaking.

She was halfway down the stairs when she heard him call her.

She stopped and looked up. He stood at the top of the stairs, an unreadable expression in his dark eyes.

"Looking for me?"

Taking a deep breath, she took one step up toward him, but he anticipated her and came down swiftly to meet her. He stepped a few stairs below her, bringing them to eye level with each other.

"I didn't want to interrupt," she said quietly. "Your mother seemed so peaceful."

"I thank you for that. She gets little enough sleep as it is – very restless, most of the time." He rubbed the back of his neck. "But she likes it when I read to her."

"Oh, I'm sure."

Lili couldn't help but think that she herself would like it, too – like it very much. His deep voice was so soft and soothing when he put his mind to it.

She shoved the thought away hastily, before it led to a blush.

"I only wanted to change the dressing on your hand."

"Oh." He lifted his hand and looked at it as though he had forgotten its existence. "Aw, don't worry about it. I'll go in to see the doctor tomorrow morning, and he can fix it up for me if need be."

His carelessness about the split knuckles made her heart hurt a little; and, too, it pained her to see him wince when he smiled, knowing that the bruising on his jaw must hurt him badly. The bruises were already a deep purple and would soon turn yellow and disappear, but for the meantime, she couldn't see them without being reminded of her silliness the day before.

"That's ridiculous," she said, a bit more stiffly than she intended. "I'm perfectly capable of changing a bandage."

He eyed her.

"No doubt you are," he said, agreeably, and then that grin – and that wince. "Feelin' a little guilty, eh? Well, all right, Lili, if you insist on taking care of me just to set your mind at ease…"

How dare he make such assumptions about her. And, more infuriatingly still, how dare he be entirely correct about such assumptions. She lifted her chin.

"If you'd rather go around with a blood-soaked bandage on your hand, I suppose I shouldn't be surprised. After all, you're a soldier, aren't you, and I expect such things are badges of honor to men like you."

His smile disappeared at once.

"Now, don't be mean to me just because I was right," he said, softly.

Now she felt guilt twist within her, more strongly than ever. She dropped her gaze from his and turned to go down the stairs. Silently, he followed her.

She gathered a roll of fresh bandages, a bowl of water, and a rag to wipe his knuckles clean of dried blood. Obediently, he took a seat before her on the settee in the sitting room and lifted his hand up to her without being asked. She longed to say something to him – almost anything – but there was nothing but a faintly uncomfortable silence between them as she unwrapped the bandage and threw it into the fireplace.

She ought to say something – she was responsible for the silence, and the discomfort – and all of this was her fault, after all. But she couldn't very well go back to the same subject and expect that they wouldn't argue about it. She had to take another tack entirely.

As she cut the new bandage to the length she wanted, she said, "It's very sweet of you to read to your mother."

Was she imagining the faint blush on his dark cheeks?

"I'm glad that you think so – and gladder that she likes it. She has little enough pleasure in her life these days."

"Is she never able to get out of bed?"

His lips tightened a little, but his voice was even when he answered.

"Hardly ever," he said. "Once in a great while – Christmas morning, I think, was the last time. And in the first week of September, she ventures out of the house to my father's grave to mark the anniversary of his passing."

"She must have loved him very much."

"It runs in the family," he said, his eyes on her hands as she wrapped the bandage around his. "We don't love often, but when we do – we love deep."

She caught her breath; her heart was pounding. He tilted his head, almost curiously, as he watched her fingers falter.

"Reckon you know a thing or two about that," he said.

It was more of a question than a statement, despite how it was phrased. He was probing gently, she understood, trying to get more out of her. She'd hinted time and again at her past and had of course made the mistake of calling him Peter before they'd even met. He must know that she had someone in her mind, in her heart – someone who stood between the two of them, even though they were all but officially engaged.

And yet, something in her balked at his gentle questioning. She didn't want to tell him about what she'd been through; he would laugh at her, she thought, or pity her, and she wasn't sure which would be worse. She wanted him to forget that she'd ever mentioned Peter's name, and yet she wanted too to carry Peter's memory with her always. She knew it was a contradiction, and she was being unreasonable, and yet that knowledge did not help matters in the least.

She lifted her chin.

"There," she said briskly, and dropped his hand, stepping away. "Good as new."

He held his newly bandaged hand in the other, carefully, and eyed her for a moment.

"Nothing about me is new, Liliana," he said. "I'm old as the hills, compared to a young thing like you. Reckon you realize I've been through it – that I've got a history. Can't hardly avoid it, by the time you get to be my age. I drank more than I ought, when I was younger, and I fought hard in the war. I don't regret that – but I do regret being away from my family when they needed me. I hope you won't hold my history against me, Lili – and I hope you can trust that I'll do the same."

She took a deep breath, preparing to reply to him, to tell him that she had no history in need of forgiveness – but with a gentle smile and a nod of thanks, he turned away from her.

She was grateful for it.

It saved her from having to lie, once more.

CHAPTER 6

Orph Miller was certain that he'd never been more confused in his life.

He wasn't sure whether he wanted to take Lili Elison in his arms and hold her forever, or drive her back to the train station himself. It was clear that she wasn't set on marrying him – her prideful, bitter, angry responses to him at times proved that much. At the same time, he couldn't help but notice her frequent blushes when he complimented her, or when she caught him looking her way. He supposed that she must be aware that he thought her the prettiest girl he'd ever laid eyes on.

And she seemed determined to use that against him.

The more he thought about the events of the past week, the more frustrated – and angry – he grew. Her insistence on seeking him out in the barn loft, when he had gone to clear his head a bit; her apparent irritation with him for not coming to eat lunch with them, and then her subsequent rejection of his offer to accompany her; her childish reaction of running away from him in town and going precisely where he had warned her not to.

All of that mounted up to a powerful bit of irritation.

And yet, nearly all that irritation was undone by his amusement – and admiration – over her response to the insults hurled at him and his mother. No, kicking an angry, fight-hungry drunk and his friends was not the wisest thing she could have done. But he couldn't fault her for it, all the same. The Lord knew he was right on the verge of doing so himself.

What really got to him, though – and even more so, the longer he thought about it – was that she must know how he felt about her, and that she was willing to twist him around her little finger on a whim.

And he was so easily twisted.

And all that while she was treating him with such disdain. Good Lord – he rubbed his face with both hands. If that girl ever decided to treat him nicely, he'd beg at her feet.

What sort of attitude was that for a self-respecting man of nearly forty?

It was all his aunt's fault, he thought darkly.

The first of August had finally arrived – hot and still, but with a taste of an impending change in the wind. Lili Elison had been in residence at the Miller ranch for a solid month now, and neither of them had spoken of their engagement and potential marriage. The days seemed to crawl by at times, and fly by at others. His mother was more pale each time he went into visit her, and he knew that her time was growing short. But he couldn't – he wouldn't – marry someone who did not want to marry him, simply to ease her passing. It meant peace for her final days, but it meant a lifetime for him – a lifetime of pain and sorrow and misery, if Lili decided that she regretted her decision.

He was still convinced that she had someone else in mind. Someone younger than he, no doubt. Someone more her age. What was the story? Why had she come here to marry him when there was someone else in her heart?

Her aunt had forced her into it – perhaps her beau was unsuitable. Perhaps he couldn't take care of her. Perhaps he was promised to another. A hundred different circumstances could have sent Lili Elison on her journey to Culver's Creek, and a hundred more could make the difference in whether she stayed or returned to Boston. All of them, though, amounted to the same thing in Orph's mind.

It didn't matter that he felt he was falling deeply in love with Lili Elison.

It didn't matter – because he wouldn't marry anyone who was in love with someone else.

He carried this certainty around with him everywhere, a burden that he could not set down and walk away from. He felt it breathing down his neck as he stood at the kitchen window on the first of August, watching Lili outside on the back porch.

She was bent almost double over something in her lap – a book. A journal. He'd seen her write in it before and had always felt a sharp surge of curiosity about what she was setting down. Now, thinking of her past, he felt that curiosity stronger than ever. Surely, the answers to the conundrum must be in that journal. She must have written about the man of her dreams, whoever he was – and perhaps she was writing about him even now, so caught up in her thoughts that she was heedless of the gorgeous sunset that was spreading out before her, the skies vivid with orange and yellow and pink and gold.

On a whim, he stepped out onto the veranda. She gasped as she looked up at him, her face turning slowly as pink as the skies – and that told him all he needed to know, he thought grimly.

But he kept his voice light, amused.

"Not writing about me, are you?"

The blush deepened, and she lifted her chin proudly.

"As a matter of fact, I'm writing a story," she said.

"Oh?" He arched an eyebrow.

"Yes. A story."

"What about?"

She clapped the book in her lap closed, with a sound of finality.

"It's a fairy tale," she said, suddenly sweet. "A romantic fairy tale."

"Let me guess – 'once upon a time,' it starts…"

"And it ends 'they lived happily ever after.' Yes, I see you are familiar with the concept."

He grinned. His jaw hurt a little, but not nearly as bad as it had hurt the first few days after the fight. It was healing up nicely, and so were his knuckles.

"I've read a fairy tale or two to Ma," he said. "I think they're her favorites. You might share it with her when it's all finished."

She narrowed her eyes at him as though suspicious of his real meaning, but after a moment her tense face relaxed a little, and she even went so far as to smile.

"If I ever finish it," she said, "I will."

He shoved his hands in his pockets and went to lean against the railing of the porch, hoping that the dizziness that her smile always caused him would pass soon. He nodded at the skies.

"Beautiful tonight," he said softly.

Her gaze followed his, and she nodded.

"Yes, it is…"

He found his own gaze returning to her upturned face, unbidden. He couldn't stop the words that slipped from his mouth.

"And the sunset ain't bad, either."

Her eyes flicked to his swiftly, and he was gratified to see an even fuller, deeper color flush her cheeks. He grinned at her and pushed away from the railing.

"I hope you don't mind," he said, "but we're going to have company tomorrow."

"Oh?"

"My cousin Charles will arrive on the morning train. He'll be here for a few weeks before he goes back to college."

"Ah," she said softly, and then, "Well, I hope we'll have enough room. Wherever will we put him?"

They grinned at each other in mutual amusement, and Orph headed back to the door.

"You'll like him, I think," he said. "He's about your age. And, of course, he's from Boston."

She raised an eyebrow at him as he paused on the threshold.

"Just because someone is from Boston," she said, "doesn't mean that I like them any more than someone who isn't from Boston."

He turned away from her and smiled faintly.

"Doesn't it just," he said quietly, and went inside, leaving her to watch the rest of the sunset on her own.

The next morning, he was waiting at the train station when Charles Morris stepped onto the little platform, a ready smile already on his lips.

"Cousin."

Orph shoved his hat back on his head and grinned at the younger man.

"Well, well, looks like we've got a lawyer in town. Now, you know, Charles, that Mr. Stepshaw is already providing this town with legal services. I don't reckon Culver's Creek is big enough to require two shysters..."

Charles laughed and threw an arm around his cousin's shoulders.

"Never mind that," he said. "I reckon Ma will want to hear all about college and Mr. Partridge, too, so unless you want to hear all my stories at least twice, we'd better change the subject. Say, what about you, Orph? Ma said your young bride arrived last month. Am I too late? Did I miss the wedding?"

"You know your ma would have never stood for such a thing. No, we're not married yet – don't even have a date set for the ceremony."

"No? Why not?" Charles wheeled on him, squinting. "You're not getting cold feet, are you?"

Orph eyed his younger cousin, his mind whirling. He was reluctant to tell Charles that he wasn't sure whether he and Lili would ever be married – but he wasn't sure why he was so hesitant. He and his cousin had grown up together, inasmuch as two men twelve years apart can grow up together, and they'd never had any secrets. And yet – perhaps it was that he had a sneaking suspicion that Lili would take to his cousin like a duck to water. Charles was a good-looking boy, and much closer to her age – and, most importantly, he lived in Boston. Why, if Aunt Liza had taken it into her head to marry her son off instead of her nephew, Lili may not have ever had to leave Boston to begin with.

No, he wasn't keen on telling Charles that there was trouble in paradise.

Instead, he said, "No cold feet from me, Charles – it's August, you know. Anyhow, you're right. She is very pretty, and very young, too. Ah, you'll meet her at the house – there's no point trying to describe her to you."

"No?" said Charles, tilting his head curiously. "Save your blushes, then, Orph. If she can fluster you that easily, I reckon you'll be married before September."

Liza was delighted to have her son home for a visit, of course; and, like a good nephew, Charles went upstairs right away to say hello to his aunt Rose. It was as they were stepping back out of her room, letting her get some much-needed rest, that Lili emerged from her own room.

For a moment, they all stood perfectly still. Orph dragged his gaze from Lili – she seemed politely interested, no more, he was relieved to see – to Charles, feeling rather anxious to discern his cousin's reaction to the woman he was engaged to marry. But what he found puzzled him: though Charles ran an appreciative gaze over Lili's pretty face, it was almost immediately followed by a faint frown, as though he was trying to figure something out but could not quite put his finger on it.

"Lili," Orph said. "This is my cousin. Charles, this is Liliana Elison."

Charles nodded and held out a hand to her. As she took it politely, he scrutinized her closely.

"I reckon we've met," he said. "Ma said you were from Boston. I think we've run into each other a time or two."

"Do you think so? I suppose it's possible. Liza did say that you are working at the office of a friend of mine – Mr. Partridge."

Charles nodded. His gaze was still on her, and very direct, as though he was searching for something he could not find.

"Yes – Mr. Partridge is very kind, isn't he?"

"Very," she said, and she gave him a vague smile. "I'm pleased to meet you, I'm sure, Mr. Morris…"

"Please call me Charles."

"Charles. I'm sorry I don't recall meeting you, I suppose that's very impolite of me. But I'm glad that you're here for a visit, for I'm sure that it must make your mother very happy." She glanced downstairs. "And speaking of your mother, I really must go and help her with supper. If you'll excuse me…"

She nodded to Charles, cast a swift and slightly mischievous glance to Orph, and went downstairs, tossing her head. Once she was out of hearing range, Charles gave a slight whistle.

"You know her?" Orph blurted out. "You met her in Boston?"

"Just once – a few months back, in the spring. I went to the wedding of a friend of mine. Gerald Hapstay – Hapstay Manufacturing, you know."

"Sure," said Orph with a shrug; he had no idea who his cousin was referring to, but he was too distracted to bother trying to find out.

"Well, Miss Liliana was a close friend of Gerald's blushing bride. I say I met her – we didn't speak."

"What? Why not?"

"Oh, I wanted to," Charles assured him. "I noticed her right away – she was the prettiest girl in the room. And it was a big room." He gave a faint sigh. "I asked a friend of mine about her, hoping for an introduction, but he point blank refused. Abel Thompkins, his name was, and he said she was quite a piece of work. He had tried to court her, and she as good as told him that he was wasting her time. Now, Abel's tried to court just about every girl who crosses his path, so I decided to take his story with a grain of salt – but his mother backed him up. She had been engaged a few years before, and the fellow died unexpectedly. Some sort of fever that just swept him off his feet, or something like that. All unexpected, you know.

Well, this girl was evidently convinced that she wasn't just a bride left at the altar, but a grieving widow, for she wouldn't allow any man to so much as smile at her without telling him off." He scratched the back of his head, wincing slightly in sympathy. "Even Mr. Partridge, my boss – an old friend of the family, she says, so perhaps she didn't tell him off quite so strenuously, but – well, Abel's ma told me in confidence

74

that he had asked her aunt permission to court her, and been denied. Not by the aunt. By Miss Liliana herself, though a better man than John Partridge could not be found – and rich, to boot." He glanced over at Orph and seemed to relent. "That's all, Orph – I mean, it's just a surprise, to hear a story like that and then come here and find that this girl is engaged to my cousin. I'm – I'm sure it's all right and proper, if the matrimonial agency made the match. It's just – well, it's a surprise, that's all."

"Do you know the name of the man she was engaged to?" Orph asked quietly. He felt suddenly very removed from it all.

Charles squinted up his face a little, thinking.

"Allbright," he said suddenly, snapping his fingers. "Peter Allbright."

Orph nodded slowly, letting out a long, slow breath.

"That's what I reckoned," he said.

In something of a haze, he followed Charles downstairs again, only half-listening to his cousin's chatter. Charles preceded him into the kitchen, and Orph found himself lagging, reluctant to enter the cheerful room where he had spent so many of his happiest hours. So, Lili had been forced into accepting the offer of the matrimonial agency after all – and from the sound of it, it must have been greatly against her will. If she turned down all the men in Boston, out of love for the one who had died, what chance did a poor sap like Orpheus Miller have to win her affection?

He found himself standing near the open door of the sitting room. Reflexively, he glanced in – and his heart skipped a beat or two. She had left her diary on the little writing table beneath the window. It was sitting there, alone, unguarded, and enticing.

If he could only see what she had written about him – or about this Peter Allbright...

If he could only set his mind at ease, one way or another. Then he would know what to do.

Holding his breath, he slipped into the room and shut the door just to. Then he advanced on the book. He felt sick to his stomach; this was a violation of her privacy, and she didn't deserve to be treated this way. But he couldn't simply ask her – he'd tried that. He'd done his best. There was no other way.

He lifted the cover of the diary, and his heart stopped.

There was a photograph just inside, pressed, and glued, with dried flowers atop it, like some sort of shrine. The features of the man were strangely familiar, and he squinted at it, bending low over the table, trying to discern where he might have met him – but then he realized why. The fellow in the photograph had dark hair, dark eyes, and rather strong, determined features. His lips were well-cut, his chin round, his face rather narrow.

He looked a great deal like Orph himself.

Orph dropped the cover of the journal and stepped back. Without hesitating, he went out of the room and toward the front door. He needed time to think. He needed space to himself. The cheerful laughter of his aunt and his cousin echoed from the kitchen; from Lili, he heard only a faint, fond murmur.

He closed the door behind him.

The photo must be of Peter Allbright. He knew it in his soul, without question or doubt. The photo was of Peter Allbright, and he understood now why Lili had, for just a moment, thought that they were one and the same. It was a superficial resemblance, really, but she must have been fueled by her desire and her longing and her love.

For she must truly still love him, this Peter.

And Orph would be damned if he would compete with a dead man.

CHAPTER 7

"And then I told him, Listen, sonny boy, you'd better go in there and catch that mouse before your father comes home."

Lili shook her head, smiling.

"And did he?"

"Oh, of course he did." Liza laughed and resumed mixing the cake batter. "But he didn't do away with it like I asked him to, oh no. That silly boy of mine made a pet of it."

"No."

"Oh, yes. Next thing I know, he's coming to the supper table and there's that mouse on his shoulder, sitting up and begging as politely as you please."

Lili couldn't help but laugh. The entire day had an aura of celebration, and she put it down to Charles' visit home. Liza had been even more jovial and engaging than usual, and Rose had sat up on her own, so as to better hear her nephew's stories. It was Rose who had suggested that Liza bake her son's favorite cake. The men had disappeared after breakfast, while Lili and Liza got to work in the kitchen. From the sound of it, Charles had had more scrapes and mischiefs to his name than any other boy Lili had ever known.

"Orph must have seemed like a perfect angel compared to his harum-scarum cousin," she ventured now. "I never hear stories about what he was like as a boy."

Liza rolled her eyes.

"Oh, I've no doubt that he had a few tales of his own," she said. "But then, he was half grown by the time my husband and I came to live with Rose and Patrick. He was a bit of a rebel as he got older – took up with the wrong crowd and got himself in trouble with the local sheriff more than once. I think it was sheer shame over it that made him sign up for the army. Of course, his parents were proud of him, though his ma wept every night after he first went away." She shook her head a little, smiling faintly. "She missed him terribly, but she would never tell him so in her letters. Not wanting to make him feel guilty, you know. Orph made some mistakes when he was a younger man, but he was always a good man,

through it all. He wanted to make up for it, I reckon. In fact –
I reckon he still does."

Lili rolled out the pie crust with her hands, quiet for a
moment, thinking.

"He'll make a good father, someday," she said softly.

Liza shot her a sharp glance, and then softened.

"I believe you're right about that," she said. "Anyhow, maybe
Charles can tell you some stories about the mischief the two
of them got into when they were younger. Of course, Orph
was twelve when Charles was born, but he took my boy
under his wing as though he were his own little brother. No
doubt Charles has some yarns to spin – and it'll keep us all
entertained while Orph is gone at any rate."

Lili looked up sharply at this.

"What do you mean, while Orph is gone?"

Liza bit her lip and hesitated, then let the words break free.

"Oh, he didn't want me to tell you – I suppose I should say I
just forgot, but myself, I don't think it's right. He's going
away for a bit. He's leaving this afternoon."

"A bit? How long is a bit?"

Liza shook her head.

"A week or so," she said. "I'm not sure."

"Where is he going?"

"I don't know."

"But why? Why is he going away?"

"I reckon," said Liza, patiently, "that if you run out to the barn right now, you'll be able to ask him yourself."

Lili didn't allow herself a second thought. Without pausing to reflect on why this news filled her with alarm, she pushed away from the table, wiping her hands on her apron. The kitchen door was open, and she rushed through it. Once off the back porch, she began to run toward the barn.

Charles was standing just outside the barn. When he saw her coming, he gave a faint smile and a nod, then strode away, hands in his pockets, whistling.

Orph was inside, saddling the horse.

She practically skidded to a stop before him, her hands at her throat. For a moment, the two simply stared at each other, sending silent messages – why are you doing this? Where are you going? What's wrong?

And from Orph – there was nothing more than a murmur.

She caught her breath at last.

"Liza said you were leaving."

He turned away from her, frowning.

"I reckoned she probably would."

"Where are you going, Orph?"

He gave a slight shrug. "Just away for a bit. To visit a friend in town."

"In Culver's Creek? Why not just go for the day, then? You could go and visit him now and still be back for supper…"

Orph shook his head.

"Not in Culver's Creek," he said. "Over in Brixton – a few hours from here at a fast gallop. I've been meaning to call on him for a while. We grew up together, and I haven't seen him since I joined the army. Never met his youngest son. It's about time, I reckoned."

"Even though your cousin is here visiting?" she said. Orph shrugged one shoulder, still not looking at her.

"Charles understands," he said. "He'll still be here when I get back."

"Oh," she said softly. She twisted her fingers together, wishing that she could think of something to say – wishing that she could say exactly what was in her heart. But her heart was stubborn and would not translate its feelings into words. She wanted so desperately to say something, and yet she could not. "How long will you be gone?"

"Dunno. A week, maybe."

"A week…"

Suddenly, a week seemed like a very long time.

And just as suddenly, she felt a flush of shame. He glanced over at her, and then quickly away, and she felt as though she had been dismissed. He had summed her up, decided he wasn't particularly interested, and was ready to go about his business. He had decided, she was suddenly certain, that he didn't want to marry her at all.

With the shame came the familiar feeling of bitter resentment.

How dare he turn his back on her.

She lifted her chin, determined not to ask any more questions, or to grovel any longer. For it certainly felt a great deal like groveling – she felt as though every word out of her mouth had been nothing less than a plea not to go, not to leave her behind. And she didn't like it, not one bit.

"Well, then," she said. "I do hope you have a thoroughly enjoyable time with your friend over in – Brixton. I will keep an eye on your mother."

This got his attention. He looked up at her and fixed her with his dark gaze for a long moment. Then, finally, he smiled. There was a fondness in his eyes now that made her feel a little dizzy. Oh, why on earth couldn't she simply settle down and make up her mind to feel one way or the other

about this man? All this back and forth was making her
seasick.

"I'd be grateful if you did," he said. "If you think of it – well,
she likes to be read to."

"By you, she does," Lili said.

Orph shook his head.

"She likes to hear stories from anyone," he said. "Just
remember, her favorite ones all begin with 'once upon a
time' and end with 'happily ever after.'" He straightened up
and took the reins in one hand, smoothing his other over the
horse's velvety nose. "Look after yourself, Lili," he said softly,
without looking at her.

Her heart gave a desperate leap at the sadness in his voice.
But she still could not train it to say what it felt without fear.

Instead, she said, "You as well, Orpheus."

And then he was astride the horse...

...and then he was gone.

The rest of the day seemed to creep by at a snail's pace. She
helped out in the kitchen, and threw herself into cleaning the
house, scrubbing it within an inch of its life. Liza baked the
cake and Lili iced it; they had it later, after supper, but the
time between breakfast and supper lasted at least three years,
by Lili's accounting. The weather was stiflingly hot. Even the
dogs were moping around. Charles's stories were humorless

and dull; Liza was listless and quiet; and Rose, each time Lili looked in on her, was sleeping. She couldn't bring herself to interrupt the poor woman; she needed all the sleep she could get.

The next day, Lili told herself firmly, would be better.

But the next day was somehow even worse. Everything moved so slowly that it was as though the entire world was encased in molasses. Liza grew fretful and argued with her son; the ranch hands quit work early, blaming the heat, and went home right after the noon meal, leaving the ranch silent as a grave. And Rose, once more, slept through it all.

Was she more ill than she had been, Lili wondered with a dart of fear. Should someone send for Orph? He would never forgive himself if he was gone when his mother passed, especially since he had missed his father's passing years earlier.

But when she ventured as much to Liza, she only shook her head.

"It's the heat, that's all," she said. "I reckon all of us wish we could sleep through this heat. Let her be, Lili – she's all right."

And so Lili did, though her worry over the elderly woman continued.

On the third day, the heat continued to build. Lili had never felt so fractious in her life. Was this what the ranch was like, when Orph was away from home? If so, she didn't like it. She didn't miss him, she told herself firmly – it wasn't that at all. No, it was something else.

She wasn't sure what.

But something else, undoubtedly.

At last, she managed to catch Rose awake. The frail woman lay with her head turned toward the window, watching the play of clouds outside. It was somehow bright and dark simultaneously, and Lili wondered whether it was possible that a storm could be moving in. She hoped it was; anything to break this relentless, insufferable, utterly still heat.

She knocked on the door, and Rose turned to look at her. She managed a smile, and Lili smiled back.

"Hello, Rose – how are you?"

She knew it was a silly question. The older woman's thin face was drawn with her pain. And yet, after a moment, she heard the response.

"I'm quite well, Lili – only a little warm. I reckon everyone feels the same way, though."

Lili chuckled as she sat down beside the bed.

"I reckon so, too," she said. "I know I do. Is it any cooler over in Brixton? I suppose Orph must feel the heat there, too."

"No – no cooler in Brixton, as I recall."

Lili sighed.

"Oh, well," she said. "I guess it won't make him hurry back any faster, if it's the same heat here as it is there. Rose – I wondered...would you like me to read to you?"

Suddenly, now that the time had come to ask the question, she felt strangely shy. She'd had precious little conversation with Rose, the mother of the man she was supposed to marry. This frail, pale, wan little woman, dwarfed by the iron bedstead, was to be her mother-in-law. It seemed almost impossible, sitting here beside her; Rose seemed more like an elven creature, something outside of humanity, not part of the human race at all. She seemed like a will o' the wisp, here one moment and gone the next. She understood Orph's fierce protectiveness of his mother, his tenderness toward her; she seemed so direly in need of being cared for.

And yet, there was a spark in her deep-set dark eyes that Lili recognized. She had often seen it in her son's eyes, too.

The faint, dry voice came at last.

"I would love to hear you read to me, Lili. I do love a good fairy tale."

Lili smiled, blushing. She set the book in her hand onto her lap and patted absently at the cover.

"Well," she said. "Tell me what you think of this one."

Opening her diary, she cleared her throat.

"Once upon a time," she started, and then began to read.

She changed the names, of course; she couldn't bring herself to do otherwise. It was too painful, she told herself, to speak of Peter by his true name. And then, of course, when it came to Orph's introduction into the story, she had to call him something else entirely. Herself, she had no need to alter; telling the story as it was written, bar some of the details, it was in the first person, as her diary entries always were. She found herself blushing as she read through some of them – and laughing at herself while she read others. Goodness, but she did have a flair for the dramatic. Aunt Hester had tried to warn her…

The long, hot afternoon passed, a creeping second at a time. And finally, Lili drew close the end. She reached the last entry, the one she had written that very morning.

It seems impossible to believe that it's been such a short time since he went away – and even more impossible to fathom that his absence makes it feel as though the center of my world has disappeared. And yet, it's nothing short of the truth. I am bereft, at loose ends, at a loss – it seems as though I am a stranger to myself. How can this be, when I don't yet know for certain how I feel – whether I long for him only because he reminds me so of what I've lost, or if, as I begin to suspect – I love him?

She broke off, unable to speak the final words, and wiped the tears from her eyes. Glancing up, she was grateful to see that it appeared Rose had drifted back to sleep. She took a moment to compose herself, and then closed the diary softly.

"If I love him, my past is lost to me," she quoted softly. *"And if I don't – will I not then lose my future? Oh, if only I could decide which is stronger: my love for Orph or my sheer stubbornness."* She smiled faintly. "If Aunt Hester were here, what would she say?" She shook her head. "She'd say that 'only time will tell, my dear – only time will tell.'" She heaved a sigh. "Goodness, she's thousands of miles away and yet she *still* insists on always being right."

Pressing a light kiss to Rose's forehead, she left her there to sleep and went out, carrying her diary under her arm.

She did not notice that the photograph had slipped from between the pages.

CHAPTER 8

The week went on as it had begun, crawling by in heat and stillness. Each day, the clouds on the horizon built up, bringing a thin hope of a rainstorm to break the heavy air. And each day, the clouds dissipated, or went to the north instead of straight overhead, and hope died another death.

At long last, the week had gone by. It was August fourteenth, and Lili had been in Culver's Creek for a month and a half. She awoke that morning with a strange feeling of excitement hanging low in her belly, as though something was on the horizon, something she could not quite see, but which she could feel acutely in her very bones. Today was the day that Orph came home.

Today, she decided, she would find out the truth.

She was tired of waiting for him – and for herself – to make up his mind. She was impatient with both of them. If he wasn't going to tell her straight out how he felt, then she would have to make up his mind for him. She wasn't sure how she would do it; she only knew that it was a necessity. She'd waited long enough, and the days of her life were crawling by. She had come here for a reason. Either she would get married, or she would turn around and go back to Massachusetts and spend the rest of her life as a spinster with Aunt Hester and Adam and his wife in their little house in Prestonville.

She didn't want to.

But whatever happened, whichever way things went, she had to know, and she had to know today.

She waited by the window in her bedroom, despite the heat in the upper part of the house. She saw the dust rising from his horse's hooves before anything else. She was down the stairs and out the front door before he was even in view. When he rode up before the house, she was waiting at the garden gate, hands clamped onto the pickets, eyes burning into him.

Orph reined the horse in and looked down at her. She stared back up at him. They were quiet for a moment.

"Nothing happened, did it?" he asked suddenly, and she knew that his first thought had been for his mother. She felt a spurt of jealousy, followed immediately by a sense of shame. Of course, he should think first of his mother – poor Rose. But perhaps if he had really thought enough of her, he wouldn't have gone away to begin with.

He was still waiting for a reply.

"Nothing happened," she said, shaking her head. "Everyone is fine, Orph. Did you – did you enjoy your time away?"

He ought to have since he felt the need to take it. And yet, at the same time, she hoped desperately that he said no. He shouldn't have enjoyed a moment of it; he should have been wrapped up in thoughts of her, and their engagement, and their wedding, as she had been. She hoped the moments had crawled by for him as slowly as they had done for her.

But he only made an equivocal face, as though that were neither here nor there.

"Michael's younger son is named Clayton," he ventured. "He told me they had thought of naming him after me, but his wife wouldn't have it."

Lili caught herself smiling, despite herself.

"I'm not surprised," she said. "Anyhow, there really can only be one Orpheus."

"Hmph," said Orph, distantly. He slid down from the saddle and took the reins in hand. "I'd better brush Trixie here down and let her have her oats. It's going to storm any minute."

While Lili was looking hopefully at the swirling skies, he led the horse toward the barn. She hesitated for a long moment, watching after him; but her patience was at an end, and she was through the gate and following in his wake before she allowed herself a second thought.

He glanced over his shoulder.

"You're not going to offer me a sandwich and a lecture because I missed lunch, are you?"

Lili chuckled – and then caught herself and frowned.

"No," she said. "I have no sandwich – and I have no lecture. But I would like to talk to you, Orph."

Orph gave a faint smile that did not quite reach his eyes.

"Good," he said. "I'd like to talk to you too."

They stepped into the barn, and he turned around to face her abruptly, raising a hand to cut her off as she opened her mouth to speak.

"I've made a decision," he said. His voice was soft, but definite; there was no question, no room for doubt. She held her breath. "I'm cutting our engagement off. I'm setting you free – free to return to Boston if you like. I know you don't have a living situation there, but I've spoken to Charles about it. He says he's certain that his employer will help you find a place to live, and a position, if you'd like."

It felt as though the ground had leapt up from underneath her feet and was now hovering about her head, looming, impersonal. She stared at him, her mouth dry.

"Orph..." she managed. "But...why?"

His eyes were infinitely sad, and in response she felt tears prick at the back of her eyes, too.

"I think you know why," he said.

She shook her head, tight little shakes as though she couldn't control them. She had considered herself strong, ready for anything, whatever he might say. She knew now that she was far from strong – she was weak. Orph had made her weak; Orph and her love for him. He had taken a woman who was so confident in herself and her own feelings that she could turn down the offer of every man in Boston and made her a trembling statue in a horse barn in Missouri.

"Orph..."

"It's no use talking it over," he said, turning away from her. For the first time, she heard in his soft voice an edge of bitterness – the way she herself had so often spoken. It was like someone walking over her grave; it gave her the shivers. What had happened to this man that he had given up so utterly on the idea of love – that he was so willing to turn his back on her?

Despite herself, she found his name slipping from her lips one last time.

"Orph…"

He lifted his head but wouldn't look at her.

"It's over, Miss Elison," he said. "You're free of me. Free to keep your love for whomever you choose."

Lili stood stock-still for a moment, while a frigid wave of shock rolled over her, endless as the sea. Then she gathered herself and lifted her chin. The pride and stubbornness that had sustained her for so long returned in a rush, and she felt a familiar sensation that she had not felt in some time.

"I suppose I was right all along," she said. "Right to believe that love only came once in a person's lifetime. I had hoped, for a brief moment, that I could be proven wrong – but there's no way to prove the truth a lie. I'm glad I met you, Orpheus Miller – glad that you were the one to show me the rightness of my ways."

She turned on her heel and rushed out into the thick, gloomy air. Finally, it had begun to rain, and she had not even noticed it.

She was thoroughly drenched by the time she reached the house. From the end of the corridor, she heard the familiar murmur of voices – Liza and her son, chatting fondly, exchanging stories, and laughing. She turned the other way and fled up the stairs.

Moving quickly, she pulled her few dresses from their hangers in the wardrobe and flung them into her carpetbag.

She got down on her knees to pull her other belongings from their place under the bed.

Behind her, from the doorway, she heard a soft voice.

"What is it, my dear? What's wrong?"

Lili clenched her jaw and reached further under the bed, wising she could simply crawl under there entirely and never come out again.

"You were wrong, Liza," she said. "And I – I was right all along. I should never have come here, should never have let Aunt Hester talk me into trying again. I am a widow, Liza, not a bride – and I never will be a bride."

"Now, now, dear," said the voice, more softly than ever. "Never say never."

Lili edged out from underneath the bed, whirling around to face the figure in the doorway. It wasn't Liza at all.

Clutching the edge of the doorframe, swaying slightly in her frailty, stood Rose Miller.

CHAPTER 9

Lili was still staring at her in shock when she heard Orph's familiar voice from the stairwell, raised in panic.

"Ma? Ma."

He was at her side in the blink of an eye, arms wrapped around her, holding her up. Rose smiled up at him, patting his hand.

"Now, son, I'm quite all right – quite all right."

He shook his head, sparing hardly a glance in Lili's direction. Lips pressed together, he half-carried his mother to the chair in the corner and sat her down carefully. He got to his knees before her and held her hands in his.

"You shouldn't try to get up without help," he said sternly.

"My window was open, and I heard the horse – then the storm broke." She leaned forward, pressing her forehead briefly against his, and then sat up again, nearly straight. "Goodness, how we've needed the rain…"

"I would have come into you straight away," Orph told her. "Only…"

He broke off, lowering his head. Lili spoke up.

"Only he couldn't, because I had to speak with him," she said. "I'm sorry, Rose. I shouldn't have interfered. His first question was to ask after you – I should have let him go to you at once." She felt shamed beyond measure, blushing deeply. Her mother had died when she was still young, and she could only imagine how Orph must feel, knowing that his mother could enter her eternal rest at any moment – and still, he had felt compelled to go away for a week. She understood now that it was because he'd needed the space in which to make up his mind. It was all her fault…

"Mm…and what did you have to speak about, my dear?"

Lili and Orph glanced at each other, and just as quickly away, both blushing. Neither of them could bring themselves to answer.

Rose gave a little sigh.

"Ah, well – never mind. Is this yours, dear?"

Lili turned her gaze back to Rose. In those thin, twiglike fingers rested the photograph of Peter Allbright.

"Oh – yes. Goodness, how did you come by it?"

"It was in my room – it must have slipped out of your book."

"Yes, of course." She took the photograph from Rose and smiled at it briefly, then turned and slipped it into her open carpetbag. She wasn't sure why; her diary sat just beside it, ready and waiting. And yet, somehow, Peter didn't seem to belong there anymore. She would have to find a new place for him, but for now, the carpetbag would suffice. She would have to take care not to bend or crumple him, that was all… "I didn't even realize that it was gone."

"Hmm," said Rose, pressing her lips together with a smile that was almost mischievous. Orph looked embarrassed by the whole thing.

"I reckon we ought to tell you, Ma," he said. "Lili and me, we've broken our engagement. I've told her that she's free to go back to Boston."

"Oh, my dear…why should you do that?"

"That photograph is part of the reason," said Orph, nodding toward the carpetbag. Lili turned a startled glance on him.

"I beg your pardon?"

Orph looked at her, looked at his mother, and seemed to get defensive.

"Well, the only reason you even thought about going through with our marriage is because I reminded you of him a little," he said. "And for the record, I don't think we look that much alike. And furthermore, I've no intention of stepping into a dead man's shoes." She caught her breath, and he blushed scarlet with shame. "I mean – I didn't mean to say it like that. I know it's been...hard on you. And I'm sorry for all your pain, Lili, but – well, marrying me won't take it away. And I'd make a very poor replacement for Mr. Allbright, I'm sure."

She was staring at him with her mouth open, she realized.

"I – how – you – how did you..."

"Charles," he said quickly. "Charles was at your friend's wedding, and he got the whole story from another friend. I know you were in love with Peter Allbright, and goodness knows I can't hold that against you. None of us can choose who we love, can we?" He bit his lip. "But I can't simply settle for second place in your heart, Liliana Elison. No, I won't settle – not for anything other than first."

A long, pregnant pause followed. Lili's mind was in a haze, and she could think of nothing to say – well, perhaps that wasn't quite true. She could think of nothing constructive to say.

Through the silence, Rose's dry little chuckle sounded inordinately loud.

"Goodness, what silly children you are." she said, and there was more spunk and spark in her voice than Lili had ever heard before. "Liza was entirely right to make the arrangements – and a good job done all round by the agency, too. Why, it's clear as day that you're in love with each other."

The words they spoke were so similar, and vehemently said, that Lili wasn't entirely sure who said what.

"We certainly are not…"

"Not a bit of it."

But Rose was shaking her head gently.

"Now, now," she said. "Just because I'm bed bound doesn't mean I'm blind, Orph – be honest, my boy, and tell us why you went away for a week."

Orph lowered his head. He did look very much like a schoolboy who had been called up for punishment by the head teacher, Lili thought; he suddenly seemed so very young. Why, grown men in their late thirties were no different from young men in their twenties – or boys at fourteen, for that matter.

"I had to sort my thoughts out," he said. "I wasn't sure what was best to do – for Lili and for myself. For both of us."

"Hm," said Rose softly. "Well, while you've been away, Lili has been reading me a very interesting story." She nodded at the diary on the bed; Lili blushed deeply and snatched it up, wrapping her arms around it. Rose smiled at her gently. "Won't you read him the final entry, dear?"

Lili shook her head, blushing even more darkly.

"I – I can't."

"Well, then… won't you let him read it? Please, dear…" She sighed. "I can't do much for my boy, not anymore." She put a hand to his cheek, smiling at him. "But if I can help him to be happy…"

Slowly, biting her lip, feeling her muscles fight her every inch of the way, Lili released her tight hold on the diary and held it out to Orph. He met her gaze and waited until she nodded, giving him her final permission. Then, fingers delicate, he took it from her and opened it.

He cleared his throat as he turned the pages swiftly, but his voice was low and rough as he began to read.

"*It seems impossible to believe that it's been such a short time since he went away – and even more impossible to fathom that his absence makes it feel as though the center of my world has disappeared. And yet, it's nothing short of the truth. I am bereft, at loose ends, at a loss – it seems as though I am a stranger to myself.*" He broke off abruptly, looking up at Lili with betrayal in his eyes. "I don't want to read words of longing for a dead man."

Suddenly, she was desperate for him to go on.

"It isn't that," she said. "I promise you, it isn't that."

She recognized that it was an act of trust in her as he lowered his eyes to the book and went on.

"If I love him, my past is lost to me. And if I don't – will I not then lose my future? Oh, if only I could decide which is stronger: my love for Orph or..."

He drew a deep, shaky breath. This time, he stopped for good.

Rose put a hand on his.

"I'm tired now, Orph," she said. "Will you help me back to bed?"

Lili waited at the top of the stairs while he tucked his ailing mother in. He came to meet her. Together, in thoughtful, heavy silence, they walked down the stairs, listening to the pounding rain.

At the bottom, he held her diary out to her.

She shook her head, pressing it back to him.

"You might as well read it," she said. "I want you to understand – because I'm afraid that I haven't been very clear." She laughed a little. "I'm afraid I don't understand myself, so perhaps if you read it, you'll be able to explain it to me."

He turned from her and set the diary down on the hall table; then, with slow deliberation, he drew her into his arms.

"I want to hear it from you," he said softly. "From your lips. I want to hear – whether you love me, the way that I love you." He smiled. "And if I don't understand it either, well – at least we can be confused together."

She smiled up at him. She couldn't remember the last time she had felt so at peace – so happy.

"Are you sure?" she said.

Orpheus Miller nodded, and she saw the reflection of his absolute certainty in his dark eyes – along with the reflection of her own happiness.

She took a deep breath.

"All right, then," she said. "Once upon a time…"

He kissed her before she could finish the sentence. On her lips, she felt him rather than heard him murmur the final words.

"…and they lived happily ever after."

The End

CONTINUE READING...

Thank you for reading *The Look-Alike Groom!* Are you wondering **what to read next?** Why not read *The Wedding Promise?* **Here's a peek for you:**

Ray Atwell stood up straight for the first time in half an hour, stretching his back and removing his hat to flap it ineffectually, trying to generate a slight breeze.

"Whoo-ee. It's a scorcher today, no mistake."

He looked down at his employer, Shane Ellis, still on his knees at the bottom of the fence, twisting wire ends together. The job was not exactly delicate, but the protruding ends of the barbed wire made it tricky, to say the least, and the tip of Shane's tongue was caught between his teeth as he concentrated. Ray couldn't blame him. After getting stuck several times, he was practically holding his breath himself. It was amazing, how this newfangled barbed wire could go straight through tough leather gloves.

"Reckon we'll be done with this stretch by supper time, Shane?"

The younger man glanced up at him with a distracted grin.

"Maybe so, if you quit jawin' and keep working."

"Slave driver," Ray grumbled, bending back over to resume his task. "Howard would never ask me to be workin' in the middle of the blazing sun like this."

"That so?"

"Yeah. He'd have me sittin' up under the oak tree over there, with a pint of beer, a Chinese fan, and a foot bath."

Shane laughed.

"While he did the work himself, and you watched."

"Right."

"Well," Shane said with another grin, "my brother always was a little soft-hearted."

"That he was."

"A little soft-headed, too, bless his heart."

Ray eyed his young employer for a moment. He was grateful that enough time had passed for Shane to speak of his older brother without that surge of wild grief appearing in his eyes; Ray missed Howard himself – they had been friends since they were schoolboys – but he knew it was nothing compared to Shane's sadness over the loss of his only sibling. There had been a five-year age difference between the two, just enough to ensure that Shane had Howard on a pedestal. Howard Ellis could do no wrong. He was strong, calm, wise, brave, and just; all the qualities that made up a real man.

Visit HERE To Read More!

https://ticahousepublishing.com/mail-order-brides.html

THANKS FOR READING!

If you **love Mail Order Bride Romance, <u>Visit Here</u>**

https://wesrom.subscribemenow.com/

to find out about all **<u>New Susannah Calloway Romance Releases!</u> We will let you know as soon as they become available!**

If you enjoyed *The Look-Alike Groom,* would you kindly take a couple minutes to leave a positive review on Amazon? It only takes a moment, and positive reviews truly make a difference. Thank you so much! I appreciate it!

Turn the page to discover more Mail Order Bride Romances just for you!

MORE MAIL ORDER BRIDE
ROMANCES FOR YOU!

We love clean, sweet, adventurous Mail Order Bride Romances and have a lovely library of Susannah Calloway titles just for you!

Box Sets — A Wonderful Bargain for You!

https://ticahousepublishing.com/bargains-mob-box-sets.html

Or enjoy Susannah's single titles. You're sure to find many favorites! (Remember all of them can be downloaded FREE with Kindle Unlimited!)

Sweet Mail Order Bride Romances!

https://ticahousepublishing.com/mail-order-brides.html

ABOUT THE AUTHOR

Susannah has always been intrigued with the Western movement - prairie days, mail-order brides, the gold rush, frontier life! As a writer, she's excited to combine her love of story with her love of all that is Western. Presently, Susannah lives in Wyoming with her hubby and their three amazing children.

www.ticahousepublishing.com
contact@ticahousepublishing.com

Made in the USA
Middletown, DE
23 September 2023

39169902R00066